Little Lulu Learns to Quilt

Written by Tara Wilson Evans
Illustrated by Maxine Davis

Little Lulu Learns to Quilt

Written by Tara Wilson Evans

Illustrated by Maxine Davis

COPYRIGHT

Dedication

This book is dedicated to youngsters and the young at heart who want to learn to sew and make quilts.   HAPPY QUILTING!!!!!

Tara "Lulu" Wilson Evans

GRATITUDE

In all things give thanks.

Little Lulu loved to play with her momma's scraps. Her mother was an excellent seamstress, and owned her very own sewing and alterations shop.

Little Lulu's momma told her, "You are old enough now to make a quilt for your bed. You can also make small quilts for your doll, Tilly, and your dog, Trudy." Her momma also explained that, "Quiltmaking is a tradition in our family and it has been passed down from generation to generation. As far back as I can recall, we have always made quilts in our family."

Some of Lulu's clothes were too small and worn for her to wear any longer. She gathered the tattered clothing and scrap pieces of fabric from her momma's shop to set them aside for quilts.

Little Lulu and her momma used scissors to cut squares out of the fabric. Once all of the squares were cut to the exact same size, her momma taught her how to sew the squares together.

Little Lulu's momma taught her two methods of sewing. A hand-stitched method called the whip stitch sewing method. With this method, she would sew in, out, and around the edge of the fabric squares with her needle and thread. The more she practiced stitching, the faster and neater she became.

The second method required the use of an electric sewing machine and help from her momma.

One day, Little Lulu's momma had a big surprise for her! Her momma pulled a large box wrapped in green paper with a red bow out of the closet. When Lulu unwrapped the box she was so happy to see that her momma had bought her a bright red sewing machine!

Little Lulu listened carefully as her momma explained that whether sewing by hand or by machine, there were three important steps to learn. How to cut precisely; how to accurately sew a quarter of an inch seam allowance; and how to press the fabric out smoothly to make sure there were no wrinkles when sewing the squares together.

Little Lulu loved to play outside and climb trees. She tore her pants while climbing up to the top of a Magnolia tree. After seeing the tear in her pants, she asked her momma to mend them. Her momma explained that the pants had gotten too small and were too worn to wear any longer. She said the pants could be added to the pile of clothes for her quilts.

Every day, all around the house, both inside and outside, Lulu would work on her quilt with Trudy, her red Irish Setter, always by her side. Little Lulu also worked on her quilt in the apple orchard in the back yard. Before long the small squares became long rows, and the long rows became small sections. The small sections grew larger and larger.

As she sewed her pieces together on the front porch, she noticed the sections becoming larger and larger! She began measuring the quilt sections against her doll, Tilly, to make sure the quilt sections would fit her comfortably.

After measuring a section of the quilt squares for Tilly, she took a larger section of quilt squares to wrap around and measure Trudy. Lulu whistled,

"WHIRLLEE WOOT!!!"

"Come here Trudy! Let's see if this fits around you." Lulu was right! The section of the quilt fit snugly.

Little Lulu would even hand-stitched on her quilt while traveling to the fall festival with her family. Lulu and her family enjoyed the apple bobbing, festival rides, and the balloon dart game for prizes. She would listen to the music and quilt, all while enjoying the various activities.

While at the fall festival, Little Lulu's momma and daddy noticed how her quilted squares had become very long and wide! They were so proud of her hard work.

After noticing the progress that Little Lulu had made, her momma purchased some pressed cotton called batting. "The batting," her momma explained, "goes in between the top and the bottom layer of a quilt. A quilt is like a sandwich of three layers. You have your top layer made of cloth squares and scrap fabrics. Your middle layer is made of pressed cotton batting. And your bottom layer is made of a large solid piece of fabric.

Lulu's momma took her, the quilt top, the batting, and fabric for the quilt backing to Cathy's Longarm Quilt Shop. Cathy was always helpful and knew how to place the three layers of the quilt onto the industrial sewing machine, called a long-arm to quilt them all together. After sewing the three layers together she would finish the quilting process by binding the four sides of the quilt. Once completed, Cathy called Lulu's momma to tell her the wonderful news, that the quilt was finished.

When Lulu's momma brought the completed quilt home from Cathy's Longarm Quilt Shop, it made Lulu very happy. She was amazed at how soft her quilt was! She thanked her parents for teaching her and providing all of the materials needed to make her very own quilt. Little Lulu couldn't wait to lay the quilt on her bed.

After placing the quilt on her bed, she pulled out two smaller quilts she had made for Trudy and Tilly. Little Lulu had such a sense of accomplishment from seeing all of her hard work finished. The three quilts were vibrant and soft!

Little Lulu slept soundly under her warm patchwork quilt; snug as a bug in a rug. She glanced at all of the many small pieces she had sewn together to make such a large and beautiful quilt. Even pieces from her torn jeans. What a wonderful feeling to see her quilt on her bed, Trudy, and wrapped around Tilly. All of the quilts made with her own hands. She fell asleep and slept comfortably with a huge grin on her face.

THE END

APPENDIX

Whip Stitch Sewing Method

Tools needed:

Hand needle

Thread

Two squares of fabric, each the same size.

Directions:

1. Place two squares of fabric together, right sides facing and edges even.
2. Begin sewing at one corner by pushing the threaded needle through both fabrics on the drawn line. Pull the needle tight.
3. Make another stitch about 1/8" from the first stitch, again following the drawn line. Repeat to the end of the square. Your stitches will look a bit diagonal along the edge of the blocks.
4. Make a knot and cut your thread close to the fabric.
5. Open the two squares and carefully press them flat with a hot iron. You may want your momma to help with this step.
6. Repeat this process to attach the next square. Sew blocks together until you have a row as long as you want it to be.
7. Make and sew more rows together until you have a quilt the size that you want.

ABOUT THE AUTHOR

Tara Wilson Evans of Bellevue, Nebraska, has been a quilter of over twenty years. "Little Lulu Learns to Quilt" is her third children's book. Ms. Evans remembers sleeping under her grandmother's heavy hand-sewn quilts as a child. She also recalls her mother telling her of the beautiful tradition of Quiltmaking in her family. Quiltmaking is a part of her culture, and she hopes to pass along this beautiful art to others.

ABOUT THE ILLUSTRATOR

Maxine Davis of Meridian, Mississippi, has been illustrating books for over a decade. "Little Lulu Learns to Quilt" is the seventh book she has illustrated. Maxine is an excellent visual artist and often says, " If I can envision it, then I can draw it."

Made in the USA
Monee, IL
03 March 2023

28924236R00031